To Mum & Dad M.J.
To Jimmy M.L.S.

Text by Mary Joslin
Illustration copyright 1999 Meilo So
Original edition published under the title
The Tale of the Heaven Tree
by Lion Publishing plc, Oxford, England
Copyright Lion Publishing 1999
This edition published 1999 under license from Lion Publishing by
Eerdmans Books for Young Readers
An imprint of Wm. B. Eerdmans Publishing Company
255 Jefferson Ave. S.E., Grand Rapids, Michigan 49503 /
P. O. Box 163, Cambridge CB3 9PU U.K.
ISBN 0-8028-5190-8
Printed and bound in Singapore
05 04 03 02 01 00 99 7 6 5 4 3 2 1
A catalog record of this book is available from the Library of Congress
Typeset in 24/32 Old Claude

The Tale of the Heaven Tree

Mary Joslin

Illustrated by Meilo So

EERDMANS BOOKS FOR YOUNG READERS

GRAND RAPIDS, MICHIGAN / CAMBRIDGE, U.K.

In the beginning, the world's
Great Maker planted a garden.

Its different fields were each
filled with many lovely plants.

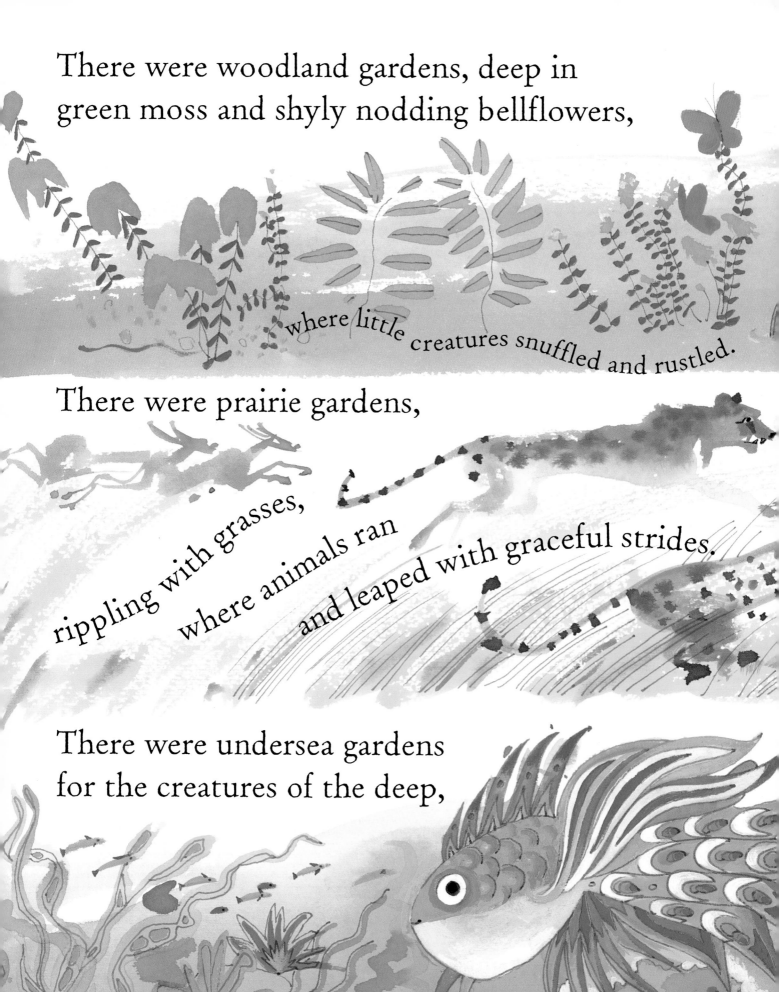

There were woodland gardens, deep in green moss and shyly nodding bellflowers, where little creatures snuffled and rustled.

There were prairie gardens, rippling with grasses, where animals ran and leaped with graceful strides.

There were undersea gardens for the creatures of the deep,

with trailing leaves *drifting* *drifting* drifting in the water currents and mysterious flowers with swaying petals.

Most lovely of all were the gardens of tall trees that reached to the sky and were a home for all the birds to live in. Their leafy branches were filled with chirruping and twittering,

twittering

chirruping

twittering

whistling,

warbling and whistling,

tumbling, trilling

tumbling, trilling melodies

to delight the world.

The Great Maker asked people
to take care of the world and to
build for themselves simple, safe
dwellings in any of the gardens
that pleased them.

But time passed, and
the people grew greedy...

"Let us build for ourselves bigger homes!"
they said.

"There are building materials in abundance,
and they are for us to use as we like."

Soon they were building palaces.

Each new
building
towered
above
the
last,
and the
palaces
were
made
ever more
magnificent.

Their thousands of rooms were filled with every kind of luxury... but the people's greed could never be satisfied.

The gardens of the world were ruined,

each a scene of the most pitiful devastation.

All the trees had been cut down.

The birds fluttered wretchedly on the cold ground, desperately trying to make new homes.

Their songs were silenced.

Then a small child looked from the top of her palace home down on the devastated world, and she wept.

"Go down to the earth," whispered the voice of the Maker in the wind. "There you will find a seed, and you must plant it where it can grow safely."

So the
child
ran
down
the
winding
staircase
of the
tower,
down
and
down
and
down.

There,
on the earth,
was a seed:
brown,
wrinkled,
ugly.

The child took the seed gently in her hand.
"Where will it be safe?" she wondered.

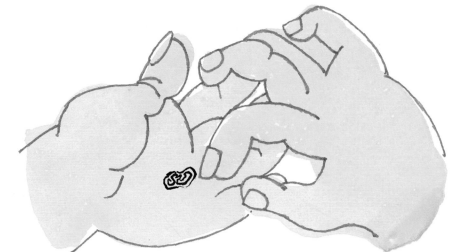

As she walked along, she came to a ditch
where dark mud oozed and a few reeds were
bending in the chill wind.

"Here, where no one ever comes,"
the wind seemed to whisper.

And there she buried the seed.

Slowly, silently, and all unseen,
the seed began to grow.

It grew into a strong tree.

Beneath its branches, new gardens began to flourish.

Soon, the creatures
gathered around it.

It grew taller than any palace,

and the birds of the air

flew among its branches

and built their nests in it.

It grew so tall it reached to Heaven,
and any
who wished
could
climb
its branches
into the
Great Maker's
garden
paradise.